The Historical Adventures of Miles and Nina

Discovering Black Inventors

Volume II

Latasha L. Bethea

Illustrated by Victor Onyenobi

1

The Historical Adventures of Miles and Nina (Discovering Black Inventors)
by Latasha L. Bethea

Printed and Bound in the United States of America

ISBN-13: 978-1-0753-9307-5
ISBN-10: 1-0753-9307-8

Unless otherwise indicated, scripture quotations used in this book are from King James Version (KJV) of the Bible.

Dedication

This book is dedicated to those who have worked diligently to get The Historical Adventures of Miles and Nina into classrooms, libraries, and other places of learning. Thank you for believing in my vision.

Elaine Clegg
Byron Cotton
Sonya Lee
Weckea Lilly

Reviews

"I learned new Black History facts that I can share with my friends. The story was relatable to everyday black life. All of the inventors mentioned in this book made a name for themselves, even with limited education. I think this book does a great job of sharing our history as African-Americans. I think readers of *The Historical Adventures of Miles and Nina* will benefit from learning more about black history."

-Faith Woodard, 10

"This phenomenal second book of *The Historical Adventures of Miles and Nina* series has giving us, the reader, a well needed "time travel" journey into HISTORY. Latasha eloquently touches on how the historical figures encountered in the first book personally touch Nina and Miles before involving their loving parents, Nathan and Sherry. This book leads us into:

History's
Impact in our community
So shenanigans can be
Told truthfully
Of our sentimental and spiritual stories.
Rich humane memories of past lives
Yearning to be expressed."

-Ms. Sonya Lee

"Latasha Bethea has done it again! *The Historical Adventures of Miles and Nina* is a page turner from beginning to end. Ms. Bethea provides a fun, exciting and relevant way to explore Black History, including believable characters and an electrifying plot. The Sutton family and their historical encounters do not disappoint. This volume is a must read for the young and the young at heart."

-Rev. Richelle B. White, Ph.D. Professor of Youth Ministry, Kuyper College

"Wow! Ms. Latasha Bethea has done it again! The second installment of *The Historical Adventures of Miles and Nina* is truly enjoyable. This time with a story that teaches the values of using one's God-given gifts to perform the improbable. The family within this novel will inspire respect, appreciation and love in the minds and hearts of anyone who opens this book. This novel shows the purpose of Black History lies far beyond the month of February. I am positive that children will love to join Miles and Nina as they embark on yet another life-changing adventure."

-Egypt Matthews, 18

"Latasha Bethea has done it again! In her second book, which details the time travel experience of Miles, Nina, and their parents, Tasha has readers on the edge of their seats with the turn of each page. I laughed and I cried and learned some black history facts that I never learned as a child, as I traveled back in time with this family who demonstrated a love for each other and a love for the Lord. The way Tasha captured these two adolescents had me thinking that I was reading a story told by my own children who display their "love" for each other in much of the same ways as Nina and Miles. Educational, inspirational, historical and biblical, this book is a great read for the entire family."

-**Mrs. Carla Bluitt**

"Latasha has mesmerized us once again! This book will empower the readers with a wealth of knowledge as they travel back in time with Miles, Nina and their parents, Nathan and Sherry, to explore the stories of several African American inventors. This book caused me to reflect on my childhood growing up, watching my grandma preparing Sunday's dinner on Saturday mornings before going to the beauty parlor to get her hair fixed! Miles and Nina with their very enquiring minds are the spit image of my two grandchildren. This is a family book; I highly recommend it to be in every home! It's funny, inspirational and very educational for all ages.

-**Mrs. Diane Mabry**

"The Historical Adventures of Miles and Nina is an engaging children's book that should spark the interest of children and even adults of all ages and cultures. The interaction between Miles and Nina is realistic, and the time travel meeting with African-Americans who had wide-spread influence on our world, is significant and memorable."

-**Mr. Byron Cotton**

We all have gifts. They differ according to the grace God has given
to each of us.

Romans 12:6

Chapter 1

Nina

After sharing their time travel experience with their mother, it was time for Nina and Miles to get their father to believe. Nina was patiently waiting in her room for the sound of her dad's Ford F-150 to pull up in the garage. He usually comes home around 7 each night unless something major happens at work that requires his immediate attention. While she was busy peeking out the window, Miles busted up into her room.

"Boy, are you crazy? What did I tell you about coming into my room without knocking?" shouted Nina.

"Bruh, chill out with all that yelling, you don't run nothing around here but your mouth. I can come in here whenever I want," Miles replied with a smirk on his face.

"Bruh, you got five seconds to get out of my room before I throw you out," threatened Nina.

Nina felt like Miles was just as aggravating as he was before they went on their adventure back in time. But she knew this was not the time to wring his neck, since they needed to come up with a game plan and support each other when they talked to their dad.

"What are you doing in here anyway, Nina?" Miles asked.

"What does it look like I'm doing? I'm waiting for daddy to come home, so we can tell him about our journey," replied Nina.

"No, I don't think that's a good idea," Miles interjected.

"Why not?" Nina demanded while folding her arms.

"First off, dad has been working extra hours this week. He is going to be tired and hungry. Trust and believe he is not going to be interested in hearing about our time travel. Plus, momma already has us scheduled to share our reports at Sunday dinner. Let's just wait, he will probably be more open to what we have to say on Sunday than tonight," insisted Miles.

Nina really hated to admit it, but she knew Miles was right. Their dad needed to relax and unwind before they dropped this bombshell on him.

"Alright, Miles I will wait until Sunday dinner," replied Nina while sighing.

"Ok bet, so have you started writing your report yet?" Miles asked.

"No, not yet, but it will be ready before Sunday dinner."

"Bruhhhh, it's Saturday; you are such a procrastinator!" yelled Miles.

"Boy, stop worrying about me, I will have it ready! Since you are all in my business, do you have yours finished?" asked Nina.

"Are you serious right now? Do you know who you are talking to? Yeah, I have my report typed, double spaced, and with a cover sheet," said Miles in his arrogant voice.

"You're such a geek, Miles."

"Whatever, big sis. You could be half as great as I am if you would apply yourself," he added.

"Get out!" yelled Nina as she began to push Miles out of her room.

"Hey, no need to get aggressive, I'm leaving. I got better things to do anyway! Plus, you need some time to get your report done," replied Miles.

"Dude, stop talking to me like you're my boss. I will have my report done so stop annoying me about it," said Nina.

"Alright Nina, but don't come to my room begging me to do your report later. You're on your own bruh," he said as he walked towards his room.

After Miles left Nina's room, she stretched out on her bed and began to recall the events that took place during their time travel. Out of all the events that took place, the story of Claudette Colvin made the greatest impact on Nina. Maybe it was because Claudette was not that much older than Nina when she took a stand for social equality. Nina felt that Claudette's boldness was beyond anything she had ever seen before from someone her age. She literally stood up to white cops without showing an ounce of fear. She was not afraid of going to jail or what could happen to her once she was there. Nina desired to have that same type of courage one day.

In Chicago, stories of injustice were as common as Asian-owned hair stores in the hood. Nina never thought she had what it took to make an impact in her community. She was reminded of what her Grandma Lillie said, "If our generation doesn't learn from the past, history will definitely repeat itself." Unfortunately, Nina was starting to see history repeat itself right before her eyes. She laid there in deep thought considering the rampant racism people experienced daily, the drug epidemic controlling the streets, the high crime rates that kept her city televised, and the horrible police brutality. Nina decided to get started on her report. She grabbed her laptop and began to take her frustration out on the keys when Miles busted into her room again.

"Bruh, you still haven't learned," said Nina as she picked up one of her shoes and threw it at Miles.

Miles quickly dodged the shoe heading towards his head and ran back out of Nina's room. Nina quickly jumped up and locked her bedroom door just in case Miles had the urge to come back into her room.

Chapter 2

Miles

Miles was mad that Nina threw a shoe at him. He thought about all the times that he could have really fought back but resisted because his father taught him that a man does not hit a woman. He is to use his strength to protect and provide for his woman and family. So, since Nina is his sister, he could not give her these hands. He had gotten good at boxing, since he had been training with his dad. Once Miles calmed down, he began to reflect on the time travel journey. He laid back in his beanbag chair as he stared out the window in deep thought.

Miles really enjoyed the trip back into the Civil Rights era and he was looking forward to the next journey. The Greensboro Four stood out to him which consisted of David Richmond, Franklin McCain, Ezell Blair Jr., and Joseph McNeil. Those young college students had a plan and made a pact to accomplish their goal. Miles understood that being black in America was difficult and being a black male was even harder. He could only imagine the thoughts that were going through the minds of those brave students when they entered the Woolworth Store back in 1960. Miles understood that they were putting their lives in danger for equality.

Even in 2017, the endless stories of Black men and boys being killed by the police greatly affected how Miles viewed police officers. The story of Michael Brown, Eric Garner, and even Tamir Rice gave Miles panic attacks each time he would see a police officer. It was a real reality that what happened to them could happen to him or even his father. Nathan, Miles's father helped him process his feelings. They had "the talk" about black men and the law. He taught Miles that the world has double standards to protect the majority but not minorities. Miles quickly understood that situations his white friends would consider minor could end tragically for him just because he's black. Miles often wondered why there was so much hatred towards Blacks in America. The sound of the garage door opening interrupted his thoughts, a clear indication that his father was home.

Chapter 3

The Family

Miles stopped what he was doing to go downstairs to greet his father. Once he opened his bedroom door, he saw Nina coming out of her room too, heading towards downstairs. Miles quickly reminded Nina not to mention anything about the trip to their dad tonight, but to wait until Sunday dinner.

Nina quickly turned around and said, "Miles, relax! I know," as she proceeded to walk down the stairs.

When Nina and Miles reached their father, he was sitting in the mud room removing his work boots. When their father saw them, he smiled and stood up to embrace them.

"Hey daddy," said Nina.

While Miles responded with, "What's up pops?"

"Hey baby girl! What's up lil man," their father replied in his deep baritone voice.

Nathan Sutton stood six feet, three inches tall with broad shoulders and milk chocolate skin. His perfect smile would light up any room. It was easy to see why Sherry Sutton had fallen in love with him so many years ago. By the time the kids stopped hugging on their dad, Sherry was in the doorway waiting to have a moment with her husband. Nathan and Sherry always made sure that their kids saw them show love and respect to one another on a daily basis. They wanted them to know what real love looks like.

"Baby, something smells wonderful, what's for dinner?" Nathan asked while hugging his wife and giving her a quick peck on the lips.

Nathan quickly made his way towards the kitchen to see what delicious food he was about to devour because he was extremely hungry. Sherry quickly jumped in front of him before he went in the kitchen. She knew that Nathan would try to dig into the meal that she was preparing for tomorrow's Sunday dinner.

"No, Nathan this is for tomorrow after church," Sherry replied. "I decided to do one of Grandma Lillie's special soul food dinners since Miles and Nina will be sharing their history reports with us. So, you will have to wait."

"Baby, I can't taste any of this?" said Nathan in a soft but disappointing voice.

"No sir, I have a plate in the microwave of what we had for dinner tonight," replied Sherry.

Nathan always knew what to do to sweet talk his wife into giving in to his request. He moved closer to his wife while wrapping his strong arms around her waist.

"So, you mean to tell me that your husband, who has worked a gruesome 60-hour work week to provide for his family, can't have a sample of this mouth-watering meal prepared by his beautiful wife," said Nathan.

Sherry playfully twisted out of his arms and stood her ground with a firm "That's correct, my love."

"Come on woman, I need some real food tonight," as he playfully brought his wife back into his arms and two-stepped to the music playing in his head.

It was obvious that Nathan was wearing Sherry down like butter.

"Alright, alright, Nathan just a little bit," replied Sherry.

Miles and Nina smiled as they watched their parents go through this little food battle. They both knew their dad was going to eventually win. They sat at the table with their father after he came back in from washing his hands while their mother fixed him a plate of homemade mac and cheese, collard greens, and barbecued spare ribs.

"Nina, honey, fix your father a glass of sweet tea."

Nina quickly got his tea while her dad paused to bless his food before he dived into his plate.

"Baby, where is the cornbread and potato salad? You know you can't have Grandma Lillie's soul food dinner without that."

"I knew you would say that," chuckled Sherry. "I am preparing both along with some fried chicken once we come in from church tomorrow.

"Oh ok, so what made you do all of this cooking?" asked Nathan.

"Probably because we told momma about us meeting Grandma Lillie," injected Nina.

Miles quickly shot Nina a look to make her shut up. Their father put down his fork with a confused look on his face.

"Excuse me. What did you say, Nina?" asked her father.

"Daddy, we met Grandma Lillie," Nina replied with excitement in her voice.

"Nina, I told you to wait!" yelled Miles in a frustrated voice.

"Wait a minute, Nina. What kind of shenanigans are you and Miles up to now?" There is absolutely no way you saw your great-grandmother. Honey, do you hear these kids?" laughed Nathan

But Sherry didn't say a word because deep in her heart, she believed Nina and Miles actually had an encounter with her grandmother.

"Kids, you know how I am when it comes to making false claims in this house. It is late and I want to enjoy my meal. So, you two go ahead and get ready for bed. We will definitely address this tomorrow."

"But daddy," Nina interjected.

"Enough young lady, goodnight," Nathan's voice was stern, cold even.

Nina and Miles both said goodnight as they walked upstairs. Miles was closely following Nina back to her room. He immediately went in on Nina, but was quiet enough not to alarm their parents.

Chapter 4

The Argument

"Nina, you had to open your big mouth. What parts of wait until tomorrow did you not understand? Now we have to work even harder to convince dad!" Miles said in a frustrated voice.

"Stop spazzing out Miles. You're just mad that I told daddy before you did," Nina smirked.

"Bruh whatever. This is not a competition! It is about us working together to get mom and dad to believe us!" replied Miles.

"It will be fine. All we have to do is show them how we opened the portal to go back in time. It will be easy, so relax little bro. And while you're at it, get out of my room!" Nina yelled.

Miles and Nina were so involved in their argument that they did not realize their quiet disagreement had turned into a loud shouting match upstairs.

"Nina and Miles, do I need to come up there?" yelled their father from downstairs.

Nina and Miles both knew that their dad meant business and if he had to come upstairs, it was going to be a major problem.

"No, we are good dad, getting ready for bed like you said," responded Miles.

Miles quickly dashed across to his room, just in case his dad decided to come upstairs to straighten them out.

Meanwhile, back downstairs Sherry had joined Nathan at the dinner table with a concerned look on her face.

"Baby, what's wrong?" Nathan asked noticing she was obviously conflicted about something.

"Nathan, baby, hear me out. I think Nina and Miles had some type of encounter with the past,"

"Oh boy, you can't be serious. You really think the kids met your Grandma Lillie?"

"Yes, Nathan I really do." Sherry reached across the table to grab Nathan's hand.

"What proof did they give you?" he asked.

"Nathan, they knew that my grandmother called me Moochie. We both know that Nina was only three years old when my Grandma Lillie died, and Miles was still an infant. How in the world would they have known my nickname?"

"Honey, I think you're overreacting. There has to be a logical explanation for this, but time travel or divine encounter is definitely not the answer," chuckled Nathan.

"Don't do that," Sherry's voice was firm.

"Do what, Honey?"

"Don't belittle my feelings and disregard what our children have shared with us." replied Sherry.

"I apologize bae, that wasn't my intention. Look, it is getting late. We will get to the bottom of this tomorrow at Sunday dinner. If your children are pulling our leg, there will be a correction plan established immediately," said Nathan as he pushed his chair back from the table.

"Oh, so they are my children now?" asked Sherry.

"Absolutely, when they are tripping," Nathan laughed.

Sherry couldn't help but laugh with Nathan because any person in their right mind would believe that their kids were definitely tripping.

"Come here, woman," Nathan pulled his wife into his arms as they retired to their bedroom.

Chapter 5

The Reconciliation

The next morning, the Suttons were moving around the house with haste as they dressed for church. Their father, Nathan, had left already because he is one of the deacons responsible for opening the doors of the church on Sundays. They had a routine. Dad left early and mom and the children would meet him there.

Miles wasn't a fan of suits, but he had no choice on Sunday mornings. But this morning was different; Miles was dressing to impress his father. He wanted everything right for when he presented his information about their trip back in time. He really wanted his dad to believe him.

While Miles was in the mirror adjusting his tie, he heard his mother call for them to come downstairs so they can leave. Miles knew that his mother despised being late for church. He rushed to grab his coat and brush before leaving his room. Nina was almost down the stairs when he came out of his room. They had not said much to each other since their argument the night before.

Once everyone was in the car, Sherry proceeded to make the thirty-minute drive to God's Chosen Missionary Baptist Church. Sherry could tell that Miles and Nina were not talking to each other based on the quiet ride to church. She knew she had to change the atmosphere in the car before the family entered the house of the Lord.

"Kids, you all are mighty quiet this morning, is everything ok?"

"Yes, momma I'm doing just fine," Nina replied while rolling her eyes at Miles.

"Miles, how are you feeling this morning? You good, son?" asked their mother, "Anything we need to discuss before getting to church?"

"No Ma, I am good," replied Miles.

"Well, since you all are having a hard time telling the truth this morning, let's discuss this argument you two had last night," said their mother.

Neither Miles nor Nina said anything, which seemed like forever. She pulled up to the next light and turned around to face both of them. Nina and Miles both knew their mother meant straight business when she did that complete turn in her seat with that "don't make me jack you up" look on her face. They had no other choice but to talk.

"Ok Ma, Nina never listens to me! I tell her to do something and she always does the opposite," Miles said.

"Miles, you are not my daddy! You cannot tell me what to do. I am the oldest. You have to follow my lead, little boy!" snapped Nina.

"Nina, enough of that attitude this morning," Sherry's voice was firm. You all can and will communicate without all of that extra stuff. Now what was the argument about?"

"Miles is upset because I told daddy about our trip before the Sunday dinner," Nina spoke a little more calmly.

"Is that correct, Miles?" asked his mother.

"Yes, ma'am," said Miles.

"Ok, kids what is your ultimate goal?" she asked.

"Ma, the goal is to get you and dad to believe that we actually went back in time," replied Miles.

"So, Nina by sharing this information last night, did you all reach your objective?"

"No ma'am, we didn't," replied Nina.

"Kids, in order for you to persuade your father, you both have to be on the same page. Right now, you aren't, which will make it harder to achieve your goal," said their mother.

"So, momma does that mean you believe us?" Miles asked.

"I believe something happened, but I am not totally convinced that you all physically went back in time," said their mother.

Miles and Nina both were excited to know that their mother somewhat believed them but needed a few more facts to win her over. So, they quickly made amends just as their mother was pulling up into the church parking lot.

Sherry was pleased to see that Miles and Nina were back on speaking terms as they walked into the church to sit with Nathan. Church was uplifting and spirit-filled throughout the service. The sermon also helped Sherry reinforce the importance of being on one accord. Pastor McLean preached a soul-stirring message from Amos 3:3. Her topic was "Can two walk together, except they agree?" It was obvious that this message spoke volumes to Nina and Mile as they listened attentively to the message.

Chapter 6

The Preparation

After service the family made their way home in preparation for Sunday dinner and the black history reports Nina and Miles had prepared. Once they returned home, everyone went to change clothes except for Miles and Nina. They both agreed on the ride home that they would stay in their church clothes. Both of them went to retrieve their reports and then wait for their parents in the dining room.

Sherry was in the kitchen finishing up the potato salad while wearing her Grandma Lillie's favorite apron. Nathan was in his man cave scrolling through ESPN until dinner was ready. This gave Miles and Nina a little more time to meditate on their black history reports while they set the dinner table.

It was not long before Sherry called for Nathan to join her and the kids in the dining room. By then everyone was ready to dig into the delicious meal that was set before them, but not before bowing their head to give thanks. Once their father finished blessing the food, everyone loaded their plates with Grandma Lillie's signature soul food cuisine of barbeque ribs, fried chicken, baked macaroni and cheese, collards, potato salad, and corn bread fritters. There was an ice-cold pitcher of red Kool-Aid to wash it all down.

"Love, you have outdone yourself with this meal, why can't a brotha get this type of meal everyday?" Nathan asked.

"Because neither of our hearts nor our waistlines can take this every day my love," Sherry replied.

"You have a point! Well, I guess I better enjoy it while I can," chuckled Nathan.

"So, kids are you all ready to share your black history reports?" Sherry asked with excitement.

"Yes, we are momma," Nina said with confidence. "I would like to go first, if I may."

It was obvious that everyone at the table was shocked that Nina volunteered to share her report first. This was not the same Nina that gave her mother and Miles grief about having to write a black history report over the weekend.

"Alright baby girl, let us hear it," replied her dad with a huge smile on his face.

Nina stood up from the dinner table and began to share what she learned with such poise and confidence. She began to share her thoughts about Claudette Colvin and how her boldness changed the way she saw herself. Now she realizes that she has the same ability to cause change even in her own community. Her report was very in-depth and thought provoking, even Miles was impressed.

"Excellent job baby girl, it is evident that you took this project seriously and did excellent research on Ms. Colvin," complimented her dad.

"Thanks daddy, it was cool meeting, I mean, researching her," replied Nina.

Miles shot Nina a look but decided not to lose his cool since it was his turn to present.

"Alright professor, let's hear your report," stated his dad.

Miles got up from the table and began to share his thoughts about the powerful impact the Greensboro Four made in their community and eventually the world. Once Miles finished sharing his report, it was at that moment that Sherry realized the work to push their children to be greater than she and Nathan was not in vain.

Once dinner was done, Sherry and Nathan began to take the remaining food to the kitchen while Miles and Nina cleared the table and placed the dishes into the dishwasher. Nina was becoming a little impatient because Miles had not mentioned anything about the trip to their father. Nina quietly whispered to Miles while their parents were not paying attention to them.

"Dude, why are you taking so long to tell dad?" she asked.

"Chill Nina, I am trying to figure out the perfect time to say it," Miles shot back.

"Miles, there is no perfect time, just say it or I will," Nina stated in a firm voice.

Nina was ready to get this show on the road.

"Nina, I got it, trust me," Miles replied.

"Alright," Nina replied as she walked off into the family room.

Chapter 7

The Proof

The family had made their way into the family room to watch a movie. Sherry thought watching Selma would be a good way to end the soul food dinner. It would allow them to wrap up their conversations on the Civil Rights Movement.

Miles quickly realized this was the perfect time to tell his dad about their journey but somehow his nerves got the best of him. Nina noticed that Miles had gotten cold feet and immediately jumped into action.

"Daddy, before you start the movie, Miles and I need to talk to you about something," said Nina.

"Ok baby girl, what do you need to talk about?" asked her father.

Their dad sat back down on the couch next to their mom, while giving Miles and Nina his undivided attention.

"Miles, tell him," as she poked him in the side with her elbow.

"Umm, we umm, want to, umm, tell you, umm," Miles stuttered.

Then there was a long pause. It was clear Miles was struggling to find the words to tell their father about the journey.

So, Nina had to take over while Miles continued to fumble with his words.

"Well daddy, remember when I said we went back in time?" I was actually telling the truth. I know it is very hard to believe, but daddy it really did happen," said Nina.

"Wait a minute, you two are still stuck on this outrageous story about time travel? I told you two last night that I did not want to hear about this nonsense," replied their dad.

"But daddy it really happened," Nina replied. "Remember you said that you would get to the bottom of it when you were talking to mama last night."

"Oh, so you are ear hustling now, baby girl, when I am discussing things with your mother?" Nathan's voice was getting louder.

"No daddy, but I just happened to hear that while I was getting ready for bed," replied Nina.

"Baby girl, there is no such thing as time travel, case closed," replied their father in a firm voice. "Now let us relax and watch this movie your mother has picked out."

Nina folded her arms in protest but did not dare talk back to her father after he used his "don't try me" voice. Miles was standing there mute. He was absolutely no help, which only made Nina's blood boil even more.

Sherry knew she had to come to the kids' rescue because Nathan can be stubborn as a mule at times. This is where Nina gets her personality from, like father, like daughter.

"Ok everyone, let's calm down. Nathan let's give the kids a chance to prove it," Sherry added.

"Prove what, woman!" Nathan shot back but immediately backed down when he saw Sherry's "don't trip on me," look in her eyes.

"Alright kids, like your momma said, prove it," said their father.

Immediately Nina instructed Miles to go get Grandma Lillie's hope chest out of the garage. Miles took off running in lightning speed toward the garage. When he came back, his dad got up to help him bring the hope chest into the center of the family room. Miles opened the lid of the hope chest and pulled out Grandma Lillie's cat-eye glasses.

"Ok, stand back and watch what happens when I spin Grandma Lillie's glasses. It will open up the portal," said Miles.

Nina waited with anticipation as Miles began to spin the glasses in his hands, but absolutely nothing happened. Their parents looked at them like they had truly lost their minds.

"Wait Miles, let me try, maybe it is not working for you because you already opened the portal using the glasses," stated Nina.

Nina took the glasses from Miles' hands and began to spin the glasses in her hand. Again, there was no action and it was obvious that their parents were becoming more impatient as they watched them try to figure out what to do.

"Ok wait, wait, wait. Maybe we have to use a new item from the hope chest to open the portal," stated Miles.

"Miles, maybe you're right," replied Nina.

"Nina, grab something else really quick," said Miles.

Nina frantically looked for something that could possibly open the portal. She moved some items around and came across a small crimson colored satchel. She quickly tossed the bag over to Miles. He did not have time to check to see what was in the bag because he could tell by his father's facial expression that his patience was running out.

"Ok dad let me try this, I promise this is going to work," Miles stated.

Miles used the drawstrings on the bag to spin it around his finger, but once again nothing happened. Both Miles and Nina had the looks of defeat. This was the only way to prove they had gone back in time.

"Are you all finished with the shenanigans now?" asked their father with a chuckle. "Son hand me the bag, let me show you how silly you look spinning your great grandmother's satchel around on your finger," Nathan reached for the bag.

Once Miles handed his father the bag, Nathan stood up to spin the satchel on his finger the same way, but what happened next would leave Nathan and Sherry both speechless! Once Nathan began to spin the bag, all of sudden there were bright lights and sounds of firecrackers. The room began to spin before Nathan and Sherry could figure out what was happening. The entire family had been whisked back in time. Miles and Nina knew exactly what was going on when they began to see the flashes of light. They also knew they had to brace their parents for the shock of their lives.

Chapter 8

The Shock

"Whoa, what just happened?" asked their father while trying to regain his balance.

Miles immediately grabbed his father to keep him from falling. "Easy dad, the spinning will stop in a minute," Miles stood there tall and strong while supporting his dad.

Nina was attending to their mother Sherry who was just as confused as Nathan about what was going on. Once Nathan and Sherry were able to focus, their senses were flooded with the hustle and bustle of everything happening on this busy street. They were surrounded by tall buildings and antique cars. While looking around trying to figure out their location, a streetcar full of people dressed for work came cruising down the middle of this busy street. Nathan and Sherry both realized, at that moment, they were no longer in Chicago. Based on the style of clothing they were wearing, definitely weren't in the year 2017.

"Ok wait a minute, where are we?" their mother asked with a hint of panic in her voice.

"Momma, please calm down. We have traveled back in time, but I am not sure of our location just yet," Nina replied.

"Wait, wait, wait, we did what?" their father asked, still in complete shock about what Nina was saying to them.

"Daddy, listen to me, we have traveled back in time. Miles and I have been trying to tell you this, since Saturday," Nina spoke slowly as if that would help her dad understand.

"But what, when, how in the world did we get here?" asked their father.

"Let me handle this," Miles interjected. "Dad when you started to spin the satchel it caused the portal to open. I think I know why; it appears the only way to open the portal is by using a person who does not believe in time travel. That is what happened to Nina and me, when I started to spin Grandma Lillie's glasses in my hand. I did not believe anything was going to happen."

"I know this is a lot to take in right now, but I am sure Grandma Lillie has us on a mission. We just have to figure out what she desires for us to learn on this journey. Miles, hand me the bag. There has to be some clues in there to help us figure this out," stated Nina.

Inside of the satchel was some money, a silver spoon, a small jar with some type of cream in it, and a sewing kit. Nina placed all of the items on the bench where her mother and father were sitting.

"Oh wow, my grandmother's sewing kit; I have not seen it in ages. She was an excellent seamstress. She would make clothes for my mom, aunts, and uncle. I remember my mom telling me

39

that Grandma Lillie made her a custom-made dress for her prom. Based on my parents' prom picture, my mom was definitely the most stylish girl at her prom that year. People in the community always had a garment that they needed my Grandma Lillie to fix. So, she always kept this little kit in her purse for emergency garment disasters such as buttons falling off a jacket or an unexpected split in a skirt. That little sewing kit and my granny's skills saved me from a few embarrassing moments as a child.

"Momma, do you recognize any of the other objects?" Nina asked.

"Not really, well let me look at this jar of cream. It reminds me of this cream Mrs. Helen Williams used to sell at the beauty shop she ran near the Carr Creek community back in Sanford, NC. I don't remember the name of the product, but it does look and smell familiar. Probably some kind of oil-based cream, Grandma Lillie used for her hair," Sherry stated as she inspected the jar and the cream in it.

Everyone looked closely at the items, but nobody had a clue of what each thing represented.

"Ok, let's see, we have money. I guess we are going to buy something or maybe use it to ride the streetcar. I don't know, maybe we are going to go eat since there is a spoon in the bag too," stated Miles.

"Son that makes a lot of sense, but why would Grandma Lillie give us this jar of cream and a sewing kit," asked their father.

Everyone was completely puzzled by the items in the satchel. Finally, Miles broke the silence.

"Well, I know we cannot sit here all day trying to figure it out. One thing Nina and I know is that we cannot get back home until we have visited all the places Grandma Lillie wants us to see," replied Miles.

"He's right." Nina added.

Chapter 9

The Sewing Machine Man

While their mother placed each item back into the bag, Miles saw an African American man across the street unlocking a door to a business office.

"Hey, how about we ask that man over there some questions. Maybe we can at least find out what city we are in and what era in time," stated Miles.

"Good idea son! Let's see what this brother can tell us," his father added.

Nathan immediately took the lead and guided his family safely across the street to meet the mystery man in the building. Nathan opened the door to the building and a little bell rung that was dangling at the corner of the door. They did not see anyone when they entered, but immediately heard a male voice from the back of the office.

"Just one minute, I will be right with you," the man said from one of the rooms in the back of the building.

While they waited, they noticed an old-fashioned sewing machine with all the parts scattered on the table. The sign up above the counter read Morgan's Sewing Machine Repair Shop. Instantly, Sherry pulled out her Grandma Lillie's sewing kit.

"Since this is a sewing machine shop, maybe there is someone to meet here since we have Grandma Lillie's sewing kit," stated Sherry.

Before anyone could respond to Sherry's statement, this tall, average built, African-American man came from the back.

"Good morning everyone, I do apologize for the delay, how may I help you all?" asked the man.

"Good morning sir, my name is Nathan, and this is my wife Sherry and our children Nina and Miles. We have gotten a little lost on our way to Chicago."

"Oh, I see, well Cincinnati is only 4 1/2 hours away from Chicago. At least you are not too far off the mark," stated the man.

"Sir, do you happen to have a map that I can look at to get us back on the highway?" Nathan asked.

"Oh yes, I think I have one back in my office, let me go look," the man started walking towards the back then paused. "By the way, my name is Garrett."

"Oh ok Mr. Garrett, we really do appreciate your help," replied Nathan.

Garrett smiled as he continued to head to his office.

Once the name Garrett came out of Nathan's mouth, it was as if the light bulb came on in his mind. He remembered the sign over the counter says Morgan's sewing machine shop.

43

"OMG honey, I think that man is Garrett Morgan the inventor," Nathan said with uncontrollable excitement in his voice. I remember reading articles about him when I was a student at A&T. Before he created the three-way traffic light and gas mask, he was a sewing machine mechanic," stated Nathan.

"Bae, are you absolutely positive that this is Garrett Morgan?" asked Sherry.

"Yes, I am absolutely positive," replied her husband.

While Nathan and Sherry were having their conversation about the mystery man, he came back to the front office with the map in his hand.

"I do apologize, it took me a little longer than I thought to find the map. But here it is," replied the man.

"Excuse me sir, did you say your name was Garrett as in "the Garrett Morgan!" Man do you know who you are? It is an honor and a pleasure to meet you sir," said Nathan while extending his hand.

Garrett Morgan shook his hand, but he was confused as to how this man knew him.

"Hmm, have we met before? If so, I do apologize but I don't recall your name," replied Garrett.

"No sir, we have not met before, but I know a whole lot about you. See, well it may be a little hard for you to believe this, but we are actually from the year 2017. You see, I was just telling my wife that I remember reading articles about you when I was a student at North Carolina A&T University down in Greensboro. Man, the money you made from your invention of the three-way traffic light fattened your pockets big time," stated Nathan.

"Fattened my pockets, what do you mean by that?" Garrett asked.

"Oh, I am sorry, it means that you made a lot of money off that invention. I believe the article reported that you sold your three-way traffic light to General Electric for $40,000," Nathan spoke with confidence.

"Wait, wait, wait clearly you must have me mixed up with someone else. But this time travel story and me making $40,000 dollars, I got to say is interesting. I sure could use that large sum of money right now. You should be a lawyer or something because you can make a story seem believable," chuckled Garrett.

"No, what I am telling you is the truth. Matter of fact you created a breathing device that we now call the gas mask," Nathan replied.

It was at that moment Garrett Morgan became speechless because he had been drawing sketches of the breathing device, but he had not told anyone about it, not even his wife.

"So, this so-called breathing device that you are saying I created, tell me what does it looks like?" Garrett asked.

Nathan began to describe the breathing device in such detail that Garrett had no choice but to believe that this man and his family were indeed from the future.

"Wait just one minute," Garrett said as he walked over to his work desk.

He pulls open the third drawer in the desk and takes out a stack of papers. He walks over and places the sketches of the breathing device on the counter in front of Nathan.

"So, is this the breathing device you are talking about?" Garrett asked.

"Yes sir it is" Nathan responded while holding a copy of one of the sketches.

"Let me tell you this, I have been working on this sketch for the last month and I have not shown this to anyone. I really don't know how you knew about my project in such detail. But let me go make a phone call," he said while walking towards the back of the office.

Immediately Nina and Miles knew that Mr. Morgan was getting ready to call the police on them. Quickly they jumped into action to get their parents out of there before Mr. Morgan could alert the authorities.

"Daddy, we have to get out before Mr. Morgan comes back. I am sure he is probably calling the police on us as we speak," Nina stated.

"I am sure he is not doing that Nina, plus I have a few more things I need to tell him," Nathan was bursting with excitement; he could barely contain himself.

"No dad, we got to get out of here right now. Think about it, you just told this man we are from the future and told him everything he has done before it even happened! We all are going to be in jail before lunch if we don't get out of here," Miles urged.

At that moment, Nathan realized what he did was something that could cause them to get into some serious trouble.

Alright son, you're right, so how do we get out of here?" Nathan asked.

"Momma, hurry and toss me the bag," Nina demanded.

Nina reached in and pulled out the first thing that her hand touched which was the jar of cream. She placed the jar on the counter and spun it around like a spinning top. Immediately, flashes of lights began to surround them, and they were taken away to their next destination.

Chapter 10

The Cosmetologist

Nathan and Sherry adjusted quickly to the second transport into time. This time the family ended up on the busy streets of St. Louis, Missouri. They had no idea of what or who they were supposed to find, but they knew that this little jar of cream would help them connect the dots. While they were walking down the street, they saw a young African-American woman carrying two large bags out of A. Moll Grocery Company. While she was walking, she dropped one of her bags, spilling all of her items. Nathan and Sherry rushed over to help her pick up the items off the ground.

"Thank you all so much for your help," said the lady.

The first thing Sherry noticed was the glass jars the lady had in her bag. It was just like the jar of cream that was in Grandma Lillie's hope chest. Immediately, she knew that this woman was their next assignment. The young woman with long, thick, beautiful, natural, black hair looked familiar to her but she could not figure out who she was at that very moment.

"You're welcome ma'am, we can help you carry your things to your destination," Sherry replied.

"That would be very helpful," replied the lady. "I am just heading a few blocks over to my brothers' barbershop."

"Ok, well lead the way," stated Sherry.

Sherry and the young woman chit-chatted about hair and skincare products as they made their way to the barbershop which was only a few blocks away. It was not until the moment that Sherry saw the last name Breedlove spelled out across the barbershop window that she realized she had been conversing with the one and only Madam C.J. Walker.

"Well we are here, thank you so much for your help. I do apologize, I was so engaged in our conversation that I failed to tell you my name. I am Sarah Breedlove and this is my brothers James and Solomon's barbershop," said the young lady.

"Wait a minute, you are Madam C.J. Walker!" Sherry squealed with excitement.

"I beg your pardon. No, honey, my name is Sarah Breedlove," stated the young lady.

"Yes, for now; but you will become Madam C.J. Walker, the first African-American self-made millionaire because of these hair products that you are creating."

"Honey, I am just trying to come up with a way to help heal my scalp. Lately, I have been losing my hair. I am trying to come up with the right remedy. That is why I have all this stuff in my bag. So, I don't know what you're talking about. Me making millions because of some hair products? Shoot, I don't even know if the ingredients I have will work," chuckled Sarah.

"Trust me, it will work and make you tons of money," Sherry assured her. "You and your second husband Charles Walker will start a business around your hair products, and you will eventually change your name to Madam C.J. Walker. I know it seems extremely hard to believe anything I am saying, but we are from the year 2017. I have read a lot of articles about you and your entrepreneurial skills," stated Sherry.

"Wait a minute, did you say you are from year 2017?" Sarah asked. "Ok this conversation is becoming a little outlandish, let me go get my brothers James and Solomon," said Sarah as she quickly entered the barbershop with a very concerned look on her face.

Sarah was concerned due to the fact that she had just started dating Charles Walker, a newspaper advertising salesman in the community. Now this strange woman is telling her that she is going to marry Charles and become a millionaire.

"Oh brother, here we go again! I know what that means; we got to get out of here before she comes back with her brothers. People, did we not learn anything from the last visit with Mr. Morgan! Miles said with a hint of frustration.

"I'll bet she is in there telling her brothers that some crazy lady is outside predicting her future," Nina laughed.

"Crazy, who are you calling crazy, Nina Marie?" Sherry asked.

"Nobody, momma I am just assuming that is what she's saying. You and daddy both have scared these people by telling them we are from the future. It is obvious that we are meeting people before they create their inventions," added Nina.

Sherry stopped to process what Nina said.

"That is true," Sherry laughed the longer she thought about it. "Ok, I guess we should go ahead and get out of here," as she wrapped her arm around Nina's shoulder.

"Well honey, it looks like we are failing big time at this time travel thing," chuckled Nathan. "We have both managed to freak out Garrett Morgan and now Madam C.J. Walker."

"Bae, I think you are right, let's get out of here before Sarah comes back," replied Sherry.

As Nathan and the family began to walk away from Breedlove Barbershop, Miles pulled the last object out of Grandma Lillie's satchel.

"Nothing left in here but the spoon! I sure hope this will send us to some good grub, because I am hungry," stated Miles.

"I am too," responded Nina.

51

"Well, we won't know unless we go ahead and spin it," replied their father.

"Honey, do you care to open up the last portal on this journey?" asked Nathan.

"I would be honored," replied Sherry as she laid the spoon on the ground to spin it.

Just like clockwork, the family was transferred to their final destination.

Chapter 11

The Chef

The last destination landed the family in the Moon Lake Lodge resort in Saratoga Springs, New York. The delicious aroma that came from the kitchen made Miles and Nina's stomach growl.

"Yes, finally a place to get something good to eat!" Miles shouted with excitement.

Nathan directed Sherry and the children to a large round table with a freshly washed white linen tablecloth. The table was near the back of the restaurant by the kitchen. The restaurant had an amazing view of the lake. While Nathan and Sherry were admiring the beautiful décor, a waitress brought them a basket of thick-cut potatoes while taking their drink order. They could tell this place was fancy, due to the attire of everyone in the restaurant. It was as if everyone was wearing their Sunday best. Miles was just about to grab a piece before his mother made him drop it.

"No sir, not until we say grace, Miles. You know the rules," stated his mother.

"Sorry momma, I guess my hunger pain made me forget my manners," Miles replied.

They grabbed each other's hands as their father led them in a short and sweet blessing over the food. Nina and Miles were both shocked that their father did a brief prayer, but quickly realized he was starving too, as they watched him load his plate.

"Hmm these fries are pretty tasty or I'm just hungry," stated Miles.

"They are pretty good son; I can't wait to see what else they have on their menu," said his father.

"I know the food is good, but let's stay focused everyone. Remember we are here to meet our last person, not to stuff our face with food," stated Sherry.

"You're absolutely right honey, I am observing while I'm eating this little snack," chuckled Nathan.

While everyone was feeding their face, Nina was checking out their surroundings. She happened to notice that when one of the waitresses came out of the kitchen, there was a black chef in charge of the kitchen.

"Look momma, the head chef in the kitchen is African-American. Do you think we are supposed to meet him?"

Sherry and Nathan both looked towards the kitchen to see if they recognized the chef's face.

"Babe, do you recognize him?" Nathan asked Sherry.

"No honey, his face does not look familiar to me. Do you recognize him?"

"Nope, never seen him a day in my life, so it looks like we will be here for a minute. I guess we have time to order from the menu now," replied Nathan while throwing up his hand to motion for the waitress to come to their table.

Before the waitress made it back to their table, a man from the table across from them had stopped the waitress. It was hard to tell what he was saying, but based on his body language you could tell he was not pleased with his fried potatoes. Then he did what most chefs hate the most, he sent his food back to the kitchen.

"Uh-oh looks like he is sending his food back. I bet that chef is not going to like that. Let's sneak into the kitchen and see what happens" suggested Nina.

"Nina, I doubt they will let us go back into the kitchen," replied Miles

"Duh, that's why I said sneak," Nina shot back.

"Nobody is sneaking anywhere, let's sit right here and see what happens," their father shot that idea down with a quickness.

"But daddy, how will we know if the chef is the person we are supposed to meet if we don't go into the kitchen?" Nina asked.

"Relax, baby girl and eat your fries. We will find out who we need to meet in a minute."

"Ok daddy. Hmmm, can I be excused to go the restroom?" Nina asked.

"Sure, go ahead, but take your brother with you." replied her father.

"Why do I have to go? I don't need to use the bathroom," interjected Miles.

"Because I said so," his father responded in a stern voice.

Nathan already knew that Nina was going to try to do something she had no business doing so he sent Miles to spy on her. At least he will have detailed information on what she did. Nina and Miles hurried off towards the bathroom, but once they were out of their parents' sight, Nina pulled Miles with her into the kitchen.

"Nina, what are you doing? Dad just told us not to go into the kitchen."

"Bruh chill, I got to see what is going on in this kitchen," replied Nina.

"Man, we are going to get into trouble," Miles replied while following Nina's lead.

"We won't if you keep your big mouth shut. Look, there goes the chef, let's get closer so we can hear what they are saying," demanded Nina.

Nina and Miles were able to hide behind some boxes of potatoes near the stove in the kitchen without being noticed by the staff. The chef was having a conversation with the waitress who brought the fried potatoes back. They could tell by the chef's body language that he was not pleased with having his food returned.

"What do you mean the fries are too thick and soft? I have been cutting and serving these potatoes this way since I started working here," the chef replied.

"I know, chef, but what do you want me to tell the customer?" asked the waitress.

"You can tell him don't let the door hit you, where the good Lord...you know what? Never mind, I will fix him since he has an issue with my food. Hand me some potatoes and a knife," as he assertively began to cut the potatoes.

The chef decided to teach the patron a lesson. He began to slice the potatoes extremely thin and fried them to a crisp. After he removed them from the hot oil, he sprinkled a generous amount of salt on them and placed them on a plate.

"Here these are definitely not thick or soft; let's see how he likes this batch of potatoes," exclaimed the chef.

"Ok chef," replied the waitress as she hurried out of the kitchen to take the plate to the waiting customer.

Nina and Miles quickly ran out of the kitchen to get back to the table with their parents to see the face of the man when these new hard-looking potatoes hit his table.

"You all were gone a mighty long time," stated their mother with a "What did you do look" on her face.

"Sorry mama, it took me a minute after I realized this place does not have indoor plumbing," replied Nina.

"Little girl don't be lying to your father and me, I know you went into that kitchen," Sherry stated in a firm voice.

"Momma I--yes ma'am, but I had to see what was happening. The only way we are going to get back home is to find the last person. I promise you the chef is the person we have to see.

"See, Nathan, she is hard-headed just like you," replied Sherry as she side-eyed him while he was busy stuffing his face with fried potatoes.

While Nina was getting a lecture about being disobedient, the waitress had just given the customer his food. The man looked at his plate of potatoes, picked one up and ate it. But to everyone's surprise-even the chef-loved them! The man began to encourage people at his table to try one. The new, thin crispy potatoes became an instant hit with everyone in the restaurant!

"Honey, those potatoes look like a big plate of Lay's potato chips," stated Nathan.

"What! So this African-American chef created the first potato chip?" asked Sherry.

58

Immediately, everyone in the restaurant froze in time except for Nathan, Sherry, Nina, and Miles. A sound came from the heavens with an indescribable bright light. Nina and Miles knew instantly that Grandma Lillie was about to make her entrance.

"That's right, Moochie!"

Chapter 12

The Reunion

Sherry knew that voice from anywhere. It was the sweet voice of her Grandma Lillie. Once her eyes began to adjust to the fading of the bright light, she saw the silhouette of a little old lady heading towards them. Once she saw clearly that it was indeed her grandmother Lillie Mae dressed in white, Sherry became overcome with emotion as she ran towards her grandmother. This 39-year-old wife and mother of two reverted back to a 5-year-old girl, while in the embrace of her beloved grandmother. The safest place that Sherry could remember was in her grandmother's arms. They held each other and shed tears until Nina and Miles ran over to join in the love fest. Nathan, on the other hand, stood frozen at the sight of his wife's grandmother.

"Nate, what is wrong with you son? You look like you have seen a ghost!"

"Well Grandma Lillie, technically, you are a ghost," Miles replied.

"I prefer the term 'heavenly being'," chuckled Grandma Lillie. "Come on over here a give me a big ole hug Nate."

After getting over the shock of seeing Grandma Lillie, Nathan walked over and gave her a hug.

"Now that we have gotten all that mushy stuff out the way, let's sit for a spell. I have a few things to share with you all before I have to go back to the heavenly realm," stated Grandma Lillie.

Nathan, Sherry, and the kids quickly took their seats so they could focus on the words of wisdom that Grandma Lillie was about to share. She slowly leaned forward in her chair to rest her arms on the table as she began to talk.

"Nathan, I have a bone to pick with you sir. I saw how you were mocking my great-grandchildren when they were trying to show you how they traveled back in time. Sometimes you have to believe in things that don't make sense with our natural minds. God has a way of using the foolish things of the world to shame the wise."

"You are absolutely right, Grandma Lillie, I never thought in a million years that we would experience time travel. Sherry and I will do our best to listen more to the kids when they try to tell us things," replied Nathan.

"Alright now, you know I'll be watching," she added.

Grandma Lillie turned her body in her chair and focused her attention on her granddaughter Sherry. She grabbed Sherry by both hands as she began to speak.

"Sherry honey, I am so proud of the wife and mother you have become to your family. I know it has not been easy juggling your career and your family, but you have done an amazing job. I always knew there was something special about you baby. Keep right on teaching these babies our family history, as well as the history of our people. After while you and Nathan will have to pass the torch on to them to keep our story alive," she said as she squeezed Sherry's hands.

Sherry's eyes welled up with tears because she always wondered if her grandmother was proud of her. Grandma Lillie had transitioned to be with the Lord only a few years after she and Nathan married and had their children. Sherry gave her grandmother another long-lasting hug.

Grandma Lillie then turned her attention towards her great-grandchildren.

"Now my little babies, the reason I sent you all to this era of black history was to show you how creative we are as a people. Do you not know that Garrett Morgan and Madam C.J. Walker only had an elementary school education? They used their God-given talents to create life-changing inventions that are still important today. Look at Chef George "Crum" Speck. He had no idea that he was creating what would become the world's greatest snack, potato chips. God has not only given all of us gifts to use for our good, but also for His glory. I am not saying that school is not important, but there are some doors of opportunity that only your God-given gifts can open. There are hidden gifts in each one of you that are valuable to society, but you have to be willing to tap into them. Do you all understand what I am saying to you?"

Nina and Miles both answered their great-grandmother in unison.

"Yes ma'am!"

"Well, I think that about does it," as Grandma Lillie began to rise up from her chair, has that bright light in the distance began to reappear. "It looks like that is my cue to head back to the heavenly realm."

Sherry was overcome with mixed emotions. She was sad because her grandmother had to leave, but joyful in knowing that she was going back to be with God.

"Now y'all give me some love so I can go catch my ride back to glory. Whew children, that place is something else! There are no words in the English language to describe its splendor!"

Everyone ran over to give Grandma Lillie one last hug and tons of sugar. As she was heading towards the light, she paused and turned around as if she forgot something.

"Oh, by the way Miles, I meant to tell you, don't waste any more energy trying to figure out why some people hate us Black folks so much! Because hate is not of God, it comes from that old slew-foot devil. He is constantly roaming and seeking whom he can devour while using ignorant people to do his dirty work. Those who hold hate in their hearts belong to him. So, don't worry about that question anymore, you hear?"

"Grandma Lillie, how did you know that was on my mind?" Miles asked.

"I told ya'll I see and know a whole lot of stuff," chuckled Grandma Lillie as she faded off into the distant bright light.

Chapter 13

The Decision

Immediately everything went pitch black and when Miles woke up, he saw his father, mother, and Nina asleep on the couch. He jumped up to wake everyone.

"We're back home everybody," stated Miles while shaking his father and mother.

Nathan jumped up with a bewildered look on his face. "Man, I can't believe we just went back in time!"

"Me neither honey, but it really was a great treat to meet a few of the Black inventors and to see my grandmother again," replied Sherry.

"Yes, it was dope and I can't wait to go on another adventure," Nina added.

"Yeah, me too sis," stated Miles.

"Nope, nope, nope, there will be no more time travel happening in this house," stated their father.

"But why daddy, we are learning so much each time we go," stated Nina.

"Because it is too dangerous, what if you get out there and can't get back?"

"Aww, dad that won't happen, Grandma Lillie will make sure we are safe like before," stated Miles.

"Kids, I have to agree with your father on this one. It is too much of a risk. So, from now on you two are not allowed to open Grandma Lillie's hope chest without one of us being present. Do I make myself clear?"

"Yes ma'am," Nina and Miles said in unison.

"Oh, and you cannot tell anyone about us traveling back in time," stated their father in a firm voice.

"Ok, dad, no problem. Nobody would believe us anyway," laughed Nina.

Everyone joined in.

"Alright, it is getting late. Miles help me take this hope chest back to the garage" stated his father.

"No problem pops," as Miles jumped into action to help his dad.

As Nathan and Miles walked past Nina, Miles looked back over his shoulder at Nina and gave her a quick wink. Is this the end of "The Historical Adventures of Miles and Nina?" ....only time will tell.

About the Author

Latasha L. Bethea, MACE, MSW, LCSW is a native of Sanford, NC. She is a graduate of Fayetteville State University, Virginia Commonwealth University, and Union Presbyterian Seminary. She enjoys writing and hosting events that focus on empowering, educating, and equipping people of all ages and backgrounds for Kingdom living. This is Latasha's second book in this series. Feel free to follow Latasha on social media:

Facebook: DaVineConnections15.5

Instagram: davine.connections

davine.connections15.5@gmail.com

Made in the USA
Middletown, DE
02 August 2021